To China, the country that taught me about life, and to America, the country that taught me about happiness—Y. C. C.

PRONUNCIATION GUIDE AND GLOSSARY FOR CHINESE WORDS

In Chinese culture, people's names often have special meanings. In this book, the boy's names convey something about each of their personalities:

Ming (Meng) — Bright or clear

Cong (Tsungh) — Intelligent or clever

Da (Dá) — Understanding or achieving

OTHER WORDS:

Ai yo (i YO) — This is an expression of surprise and excitement much like the American Oh my!, Yikes!, or Wow!

Hong Bao (hong bow) — Red bag

Nián-gāo (nee YEN gow) — Rice cake

SIMON & SCHUSTER BOOKS FOR YOUNG READERS
An imprint of Simon & Schuster Children's Publishing Division
1230 Avenue of the Americas, New York, New York 10020

Text copyright © 2001 by Ying Chang Compestine
Illustrations copyright © 2001 by Tungwai Chau
SIMON & SCHUSTER BOOKS FOR YOUNG READERS is a trademark of Simon & Schuster.

Book design by Anahid Hamparian.
The text of this book is set in 16-point Papyrus.
The illustrations are rendered in acrylics.
Manufactured in China
16 18 20 19 17 15
0813 SCP
Library of Congress Cataloging-in-Publication Data: Compestine, Ying Chang.
The runaway rice cake / by Ying Chang Compestine;
illustrated by Tungwai Chau.—1st ed. p. cm. Summary:
After chasing the special rice cake, nián-gāo, that their mother has made to celebrate the Chinese New Year,
three poor brothers share it with an elderly woman and have their generosity richly rewarded.
ISBN-13: 978-0-689-82972-7 (ISBN-10: 0-689-82972-8) [1. Chinese New Year—Fiction. 2.
Generosity—Fiction.] I. Chau, Tungwai, ill. II. Title. PZ7.C73615Ru 2000 [E] 99-462168

The Runaway Rice Cake

by Ying Chang Compestine ✤ pictures by Tungwai Chau

Simon & Schuster Books for Young Readers

New York   London   Toronto   Sydney   Singapore

It all happened one Chinese New Year's Eve.
The Chang family was preparing for the celebration.
Momma Chang lit the incense as Poppa Chang and
their three sons, Ming, Cong, and Da, gathered around.
Momma handed the incense to Ming, the eldest boy,
and he offered it to the picture of the Kitchen God.
Da, the youngest, smeared honey on the Kitchen
God's lips, so he would say good things about the
Changs to the Emperor of Heaven.

"Ask him for a big feast, Da. I am so hungry," said Cong, the middle boy.

"No!" said Da. "You shouldn't ask for things from the Emperor of Heaven. He decides who will be rewarded."

Cong shrugged, then helped Poppa light the picture so it would fly up to Heaven.

Next it was time to make the nián-gāo, the New Year's rice cake.

Momma opened the flour jar. "We only have enough rice flour to make one nián-gāo this year," she said sadly. Last fall's drought had made food scarce for the Changs and their neighbors.

"Well, I'm sure it will be your sweetest one yet," said Da. "I can't wait!"

The whole family pitched in to cook the rice cake. While it steamed, they took turns peeking to see if it was done.

"The smell makes me so hungry!" said Cong. "I wish we could have a big feast before we eat the nián-gāo."

"Me too," agreed Ming.

"Ai yo!" exclaimed Poppa. "We're all hungry. But this nián-gāo is all we have."

"Let's enjoy it," said Momma. "Perhaps it will bring us better luck for the New Year."

Finally, Momma took the rice cake out of the steamer.

"Can we cut it up now?" Ming asked hungrily.

"Yes," said Momma. But as she reached for a knife,
something incredible happened—the rice cake came alive!

It cried, "Ai yo! I don't think so!" and popped out of the pan.
It rolled past the stunned Chang family, out of the kitchen,
and out of their tiny home.

The Changs ran outside, shouting, "Stop, you nián-gāo!"

It rolled past the chicks in the courtyard. They tried to peck at it, but the runaway rice cake was too fast. It cried, "Ai yo! Away chicks go!"

It skidded by a pig. He tried to bite it, but the runaway rice cake was too fast. It cried, "Ai yo! Pig's too slow!"

It spun through the village market. A woman tried to grab it, but the runaway rice cake was too fast. It cried, "Ai yo! Away I go!"

It tumbled over to the village docks. A fisherman tried to trip it, but the runaway rice cake was too fast. It cried, "Ai yo! Water down below!"

The Changs chased the nián-gāo through the village, shouting all the way. It jumped past some lion dancers. They tried to step on it, but the runaway rice cake was too fast. It cried, "Ai yo! Watch your toes!"

Ming tried to net the nián-gāo. Cong tried to pin it with his chopsticks. But the runaway rice cake was too fast. It spun up a steep side street, crying, "Ai yo! Up I go!"

Then, whoa! The nián-gāo collided with an old woman.

Momma Chang quickly scooped the rice cake into her dish.

Da held it down with his little hands.

The nián-gāo cried, "Ai yo! Let me go!"

Da said, "Chase you so, to let you go? No, no, no!"

"Are you all right, Grandmother?" asked Momma Chang.

"Ai yo! I think so," said the old woman. "What happened? Something bumped into me?"

"It was our nián-gāo," said Da. "It jumped out of the pan and rolled out of our house!"

"Ai yo! Is that so?" said the old woman.

"Grandmother," asked Momma Chang, "is there anything we can do for you?"

"You are very kind. I'm not hurt. It's just that I haven't had much to eat for a couple of days."

"Then you should have some of our nián-gāo," Da offered.

"But there is hardly enough for us!" protested Cong.

Ming scowled at Da and poked him with an elbow.

Momma looked at Poppa, and he nodded. "Let us do as Da says. We'll share the nián-gāo."

On hearing this, the rice cake stopped trying to escape. It said softly, "Grandmother needs me so! To her I will go." Then it slowly closed its eyes.

The old woman trembled as Momma Chang put the dish in her lap. Da carefully let go of the rice cake.

The woman took a tiny nibble. "Oh, this is wonderful! I haven't had nián-gāo this good since my childhood!"

She took a slightly bigger bite. "It's so soft and sweet."

Then another, even bigger bite. "The raisins are so plump."

A huge mouthful. "The nuts are so crunchy."

And another. "Thank you for sharing it with me."

Before long, the old woman had gobbled up the whole cake!

After the old woman finished, she stood up and handed the empty dish to Momma Chang. Realizing what she had done, she turned bright red and bowed her head. "I am so sorry! I ate all of your nián-gāo. It was so delicious, I couldn't help myself. Thank you, all."

Ming groaned.

Cong moaned.

"You are very welcome," Poppa Chang said as she disappeared into the night.

"I hope she feels better now," said Da.

"SHE may feel better, but what about me?" said Cong.

"Now we have nothing to eat," cried Ming.

"Let's go home," said Momma. "I'll cook some rice." But she knew perfectly well that the rice jar was nearly empty.

"I'm cold and hungry," said Ming. Momma took off her jacket and put it on Ming.

"I'm tired and hungry," said Cong. Poppa carried Cong on his back.

When they were close to home, Da said, "Mmm. I smell something delicious."

The woman from the vegetable market was waiting outside their house. "I heard what happened with your nián-gāo. With the bad crops last year, we don't have much either. Here are baked buns."

"Thank you!" The Changs bowed to her.

Other people began to arrive.

"We all heard about what happened. Here are a few dumplings."

"I brought a fish to share," said the fisherman.

"And I brought some oranges," said another neighbor.

"Come in, come in," invited Poppa. Everyone filed
into the Chang house and placed bowls and baskets
on the table.

Poppa bowed to his neighbors. "Your generosity has touched our hearts. Please join us for the New Year's celebration."

"No, no, no," said the fisherman. "We brought this food for your family. Please enjoy it."

Poppa and Momma gestured to the boys. "You children should eat first," said Momma.

Ming looked at his tired, starving brothers and then at the small bowls on the table. "Well, I'm really not that hungry. Cong and Da can have my share."

Cong looked at skinny little Da and the generous neighbors. "I'm not that hungry either. Da can have my share."

"Thank you, brothers," said Da, "but I'm sure there's enough for . . ." When he lifted the cover off a bowl, something incredible happened!

The bowl grew larger and filled itself with dumplings!
Before everyone's eyes, more bowls and baskets
appeared on the table, all overflowing with food. The
three boys began to snatch up lids.

"Oh!" yelled Ming. "Nián-gāo!"

"Oh!" cried Cong. "Nián-gāo and noodles!"

"Oh!" exclaimed Da. "Nián-gāo and noodles and fish
and chicken and vegetables and rice!"

Momma said, "I have never seen so much food! Please,
please, everybody eat."

With whoops of joy, everyone dashed to the table. They ate and ate. They ate until they thought they were going to explode like firecrackers. Then they ate a little bit more.

When Da was too full to take another bite, he turned to his mother. "Do you think the old woman could have been sent by—"

Suddenly they heard a bang. Then a whole series of bangs.

"It's coming from the courtyard!" cried Poppa.

Everyone ran to the door.

Outside, lion dancers leaped all about. Firecrackers crackled and banged. Cymbals crashed. Drums boomed. Never had the Changs heard such a racket. Never had they seen such a spectacle. The lion dancers brought a bundle to each of the three Chang boys. On top of each bundle was a red bag embossed with a gold dragon. Untied, each bundle was a new red silk outfit.

It was the happiest New Year's Eve the Changs had ever celebrated.

CELEBRATING CHINESE NEW YEAR

A lunar calendar determines when the Chinese New Year will fall, much like Easter in the West. It usually comes in late January or in early February, on the day of a new moon.

One week before the New Year begins, the family gathers for a ceremony to honor their Kitchen God. They smear sweet honey on the lips of the Kitchen God's picture so that it will say only good things about the family. They then burn the picture so that the Kitchen God can begin its journey to the Emperor of Heaven. Once there, it reports to the Emperor on the family's thoughts and deeds. The Kitchen God is welcomed back with a feast and fireworks on New Year's Eve. The Chinese believe these acts bring good luck for the coming year.

Chinese New Year's Eve is the most important holiday for a Chinese family. Traditionally, all the members of a family gather together for a New Year's Eve feast. It is important to serve certain dishes. Noodles are served because they stand for long life. A chicken is served whole; it stands for family unity and togetherness. A whole fish is served, because YU, the Chinese word for "fish," sounds like the Chinese word for "more than enough." Dumplings, rice, and vegetables are served as well, but the last and most important dish is New Year's cake, or NIÁN-GĀO. Eating NIÁN-GĀO during the New Year's celebration brings safety and fortune to the entire family for the year.

After the feast, the younger children bow down to their elders to show their respect. In return, they receive small red bags, called HÓNG BĀO, that contain good-luck money. Wealthy families set off firecrackers and hire lion dancers to perform in front of their houses. These are people dressed in lion costumes. The dance and firecrackers scare away evil spirits and bring good fortune to the family.

For New Year's Day, it's important for the children to wear new clothes to show that they are making a fresh start. It also confuses evil spirits that may be watching. The spirits won't recognize the children in their new clothes. Why not celebrate your New Year with NIÁN-GĀO?

Baked Nián-Gāo

1 pound glutinous rice flour
   (also called sweet rice flour)
1 1/4 cups sugar
1 tablespoon baking powder
1/2 cup raisins
1/2 cup nuts

3 eggs
3/4 cup canola or vegetable oil
1 1/2 cups water

1. Preheat oven to 375°F.
2. Combine all the dry ingredients in a large mixing bowl. Mix thoroughly.
3. In a separate bowl, beat the eggs. Add other wet ingredients to the eggs and stir.
4. Pour the wet ingredients into the dry ingredients. Mix well.
5. Coat a 9-inch round cake pan with nonstick cooking spray. Pour in the batter.
6. Bake for 40 minutes. The nián-gāo will rise when done. A knife poked into the center will come out clean.

Steamed Nián-Gāo

1 1/2 cups glutinous rice flour
1 cup rice flour
1 cup sugar
1/4 cup dried cherries
1/4 cup raisins
1/4 cup nuts
1 cup water

1. Combine flours, sugar, cherries, raisins, and nuts in a large mixing bowl. Mix thoroughly. Add the water, and mix until smooth.
2. Coat a 9-inch round cake pan with nonstick cooking spray. Pour the batter into the pan.
3. Place the cake pan in a steamer over 4 cups of boiling water. Steam for 20 minutes over medium-high heat, or until the nián-gāo becomes translucent.
4. Remove the cake by inverting the pan over a serving plate. Allow the cake to cool until it's warm to the touch. Cut into wedges and serve.